The Company of Cats

Savannah Dawn

Published by Savannah Dawn, 2023.

This is a work of fiction. Similarities to real people, places, or events are entirely coincidental.

THE COMPANY OF CATS

First edition. October 16, 2023.

ISBN: 979-8215805053

Written by Savannah Dawn.

Table of Contents

Dedicated to my dyslexic friend and lover of stories, Hannah.

Cover art designed by Table Cat Games, LLC, with kitty photo courtesy of dimedrol68500172 on Vecteezy.com.

Chapter 1

Lush and green skyscrapers, overflowing with vines and powdered in a fine moss patina, towered over a purple speck on the sidewalk far below. The purple speck was one of many multicolored specks going about their speck business, but this speck in particular was a sweater-wearing, twenty-one-year-old woman named Lizina Russo, and her business involved a small detour to say hello to a cat before she went home.

She spotted his tabby coat lounging underneath a holly bush between the sidewalk and the highly decorated storefront of a luxury meat market.

"Hey, Pebbles," she called out.

He hoisted himself up. "Howdy," he called back. "How was work?"

"Long shift." Lizina smiled and crouched down to stroke her hand along his back. "A little girl called a deer a dog today." The Arboretum where Lizina worked, though a fine restaurant in its own right, was mainly designed to attract wealthy Satellite tourists with its solid glass walls so patrons could view the earth's vibrant flora and fauna while eating fancy food cooked over an open flame. Evidently, this was the girl's first time on the Surface.

Pebbles purred, arching into Lizina's touch. "What did the deer think of that?"

"I don't think he heard."

"Shame. Smug bastards."

The restaurant owner had gone to great lengths to convince the deer to parade by the Arboretum's windows on a daily basis, so Lizina didn't like to talk poorly of them. Besides, work wasn't the most appealing conversational topic after spending the entire day wiping sludge off windows for less than a living wage. She switched subjects. "I can't stay long today. I have an exam soon, and the instructor will fail me if I don't log in on time. Mom almost made me late for the last one, and I don't want to risk it."

Pebbles stopped purring. "Eugh. Speaking of bastards."

Lizina's shoulders slumped. "Yes. Well. It is what it is."

"You should live somewhere else."

Lizina snorted. "I can't just sleep on the street like you."

"Why not?" Pebbles replied with the steady stare that cats used when they were being sincere. "John does, and he seems to do alright."

"John's *homeless*." Lizina winced, thinking about the friendly man with the bright blue coat and cracked computer screen. She'd spoken with him many times during her daily commute because she liked to hear what he had to say. His stories were rarely joyous, though—that's what you could expect when you lost your grip on a place to *be* in the world. There just wasn't enough space. Lizina inwardly shuddered at the thought of being so exposed to the cruelty of the world. "And I can assure you that he isn't alright."

Pebbles flicked his tail with the same demeanor that a human would give a shrug. "If you insist. But it's a big planet. There's gotta be *somewhere* better than your mother's jaws."

Lizina shook her head at the strange cat idiom and stood up. "Yeah, and maybe I'll find it when I get my certificate. I gotta go."

"See you tomorrow." Pebbles twisted himself in one last slide around her ankles before he disentangled himself from her legs. "Good luck."

Lizina did not feel particularly significant walking among the looming skyscrapers, and this lack-of-significance only made her more worried about the exam. In a sense, her whole future career as an internet security specialist relied on it. The exam would make up twenty percent of her final grade for the class, and passing the class was necessary to get her certificate. No certificate ... no job. She drooped at the thought of spending the rest of her life scraping sludge at the Arboretum. She'd pegged everything this. She couldn't afford to go to school again.

She rubbed her thumb and forefinger against the strap of her purse and picked up her pace without thinking. The professor would give her extra "disability" time, at least. She'd hate using it, but at this point she supposed she should be taking every advantage she could get.

Her family's unit was in the center of the seventh floor of a slowly deteriorating apartment complex that gave the impression of being consumed by the city's ubiquitous foliage rather than scaffolding it. Today the elevator wasn't responding when she waved her hand in front of the sensor, so she trekked up the stairs instead.

Her mother's tan work uniform hung neatly just inside the door. Colorful letters spelling out "Joyful Gardens" bounced across the back of the airy t-shirt, and a ridged 3D printed nametag with the much more blocky "MARTINA" clung to the front. A pair of soiled purple gloves rested on a small end table. Lizina's mother was probably in her bedroom, finishing up whatever freelance work she'd managed to find online during her weekly day off from tending the plants at the nursery. Lizina's younger brother, Gabriel, lay stretched out on the worn coffee-colored couch in the sparsely furnished, windowless living room. He glanced up from his computer—a sleek, new model one could easily toss from one hand to the other—when he saw her.

"You didn't take the trash out. Mom's pissed," he said.

Unlike Lizina, he lived in the apartment for free. Because he was taking classes to become an internet security specialist. Just like Lizina. Just like their father, before he died. Though Lizina was three years older than Gabriel, he was on track to graduate alongside her at the end of the year.

"I've been at work since three AM," Lizina retorted. "How the fuck can I take the trash out while I'm at work?"

He shrugged. "Should've done it before you left."

"Before I left at two-thirty in the morning?" Lizina crossed her arms and stared at him. It wasn't his fault their mother expected the things she did of Lizina—but he didn't have to be such a dick about it.

Gabriel shrugged again, this time with indifference. "Not like you've got anything better to do."

Air steadily forced itself out of Lizina's nose. She did, in fact, have better things to do. She'd been studying all night for her upcoming exam. It shouldn't have taken so long, but she had to read each line of code two or three times before she could decipher all of the letters. They just kept . . . slipping off of the page. She knew better than to say anything about it, though. Martina and Gabriel both insisted that coding was no place for someone with dyslexia, that Lizina should focus on more practical, less academic goals. Like taking care of Gabriel, so he could get a nice job that would get them a nice new apartment with a nice window or two. Gabriel was the one with the promising future. Lizina would be accomplished if she

4

scraped by with something average. That's what all of their schoolteachers had said, and that's what their mother believed. Sometimes Lizina wondered if they were right.

Martina, apparently having overheard the conversation, burst into the room and planted her hands on thin hips beneath her billowing sweatshirt. Her tied-back curls quaked as she sharply jutted her chin up to narrow her eyes at Lizina's own, five inches higher.

"Garbage. Now," she hissed.

Lizina quietly slung her bag back over her shoulder, tucked her head, and went into the kitchen to do as she was told. She'd risk making her mother even more angry if she stopped to put her bag down in her room first.

The trip from the kitchen, down the stairs, out to the dumpster, and back up to the apartment took a total of nine minutes. Lizina checked her phone. Twenty-six minutes until the exam. Lizina hurried toward her bedroom.

Martina stepped in front of her, arms crossed firmly over her chest. "There are dirty dishes in the sink."

Lizina stopped abruptly, partly from her mother's icy glare, partly from the threatening tone of the implied command, and mostly to avoid a sudden collision. Lizina bit her lip. Their dishwasher had broken four years ago, and Martina insisted it was too expensive to fix with the cost of rent skyrocketing every year. Since then all their dishes had to be hand-washed. By Lizina, the one child in the house who was already putting three fourths of her paycheck toward said skyrocketing rent.

"I need to log on to my exam. I can do them after. I can't be late for this," Lizina pleaded, searching Martina's face for any place of softness. It used to be there, long ago.

Her mother's unforgiving eyes and rigid blockade remained unmoved. "You should have considered that before you decided not to do them yesterday."

Lizina hadn't *decided* not to do the dishes. She'd forgotten to do them while she was studying. But there was no point in trying to tell Martina that.

"They'll lock me out! I'll lose twenty percent of my grade!" she blurted instead.

Martina rolled her eyes. "Then talk to the dyslexia people or whoever it is at the school that's holding your hand. I don't care. You don't get to abandon your family obligations just because you feel like it. Do the dishes. Now."

Lizina slunk past Gabriel still on the couch, who didn't seem to notice her, on her way to the kitchen. He had always been this apathetic, even when their father was still alive. Was that *porn* on his feed? Irritation rose in her stomach, then she shook it away. Whatever.

Lizina suddenly stopped in the kitchen doorway. Her mother must have made an eight course meal sometime in the past two days, because pots and pans and mixing bowls overflowed from the sink. Mismatched plates, glasses, and silverware occupied the tired counters on both sides. She wished she'd remembered yesterday.

Lizina dropped her bag, rolled up her sleeves, and dumped dish soap into the sink. Her eyes wandered from the plastic cups to the large digital clock on the far right wall. Prancing electric cats from a free app Martina had downloaded years ago swiped at the zero in "1:40." The exam locked at two.

When Lizina rinsed the sludge off of a yellowed plate, a fat tabby cat sat on the five in "1:45."

6

While she still scrubbed at a hardened stain on a particularly difficult pot, a skinny tuxedo cat stretched out in front of "1:55."

At 1:57, a little orange kitten blinked from the side of the screen. Lizina put the last dish on the rack and rushed to her room.

Her mother blocked the hallway yet again.

"Mom!" Lizina peered anxiously across her mother's shoulder.

Martina narrowed her eyes even further. "Don't use that tone of voice with me!"

Lizina danced on her toes. She could feel the seconds passing by like little dust motes past her face.

She took a deep breath. "I'm sorry."

Martina looked up, straight into Lizina's eyes. "Vacuum the living room."

For a moment, Lizina considered arguing. Then she remembered the last time she fought with her mother, when Martina accused her of selfishly wasting her family's time and money to pursue vapid fantasies. Martina had said it was an indulgence she wouldn't tolerate in her house much longer if Lizina kept pushing her family's needs aside. Lizina believed her. She hunched her shoulders and dropped her bag in the hallway.

"Okay."

Two minutes and thirty seconds later, the living room floor had barely received a sweep of sucking air and Lizina was on the threadbare carpet with her computer clutched tight in her hands. Beside her, the vacuum roared as if it really was being used for its intended purpose—and not as if it had been left on to keep Martina from noticing Lizina's pause in her daughterly duties. Gabriel glanced over at Lizina's crouched figure with passing interest before returning his attention to his own computer. Lizina tapped aggressively on her screen. Finishing the floor and hooking the computer's mouse up would have to wait until after she logged in to the exam. She rapidly punched in her required thirteen character password for the course app. A little red box popped up.

We don't recognize that email and password combination.

Lizina gritted her teeth and punched the password in again, somewhat slower.

The screen flashed.

A blue square flipped up, expanding over the entire screen.

Sorry, this exam is now locked.

Her knuckles whitened and her breaths came out in ragged gasps. Twenty percent of her grade—gone.

Lizina stared at the plain white ceiling of her bedroom. With nothing else she could do, she had finished vacuuming to her mother's exacting standards, and now she was here.

She'd had a "B" in the class, had spent hours staring at hazy letters until her eyes ached from the strain, to get it. Would she be able to get by with a "D"? A surge of worry and rage flowed through her body until her shoulders shook like a trembling, if not particularly threatening, earthquake. She needed to pass this class to complete her certificate. A "D" would already look bad to employers, but any small slip-up from here on out could cause her to fail the course entirely. What if something like this happened again?

Her hand shot out and grabbed at her computer on the pink plastic stool by her bed. It wasn't as new, or nice, or sleek as Gabriel's, but she had bought it herself. Her fingers opened the search engine before her eyes could even register the screen. When they could, they looked into the dim black void of the search bar.

H-o-w- -t-o- -m-o-v-e- -o-u-t- -f-a-s-t, her fingers jabbed.

Of course, she wasn't *really* expecting an answer. The internet didn't work that way. It was just nice to think that there was at least *one* thing she could do before giving up entirely.

The first result was a link to a forum on an "ask" website. She clicked it. The question read:

> *Hi, I'm currently living alone with my mother in an apartment (planetside). She's kind of abusive (long story), but I've been able to make it work. Until last night when things got really bad. Is there any way I can move out asap?*

The first comment said, *You can always move in with me bb ;).* Lizina did not think it helpful to either the original asker or herself. The second, *Have you tried looking for your own apt or moving in with friends??* made her stop and think. Aside from Pebbles, she'd only interacted with her own friends online since grade school. She couldn't just... up and *ask* to move in with them.

She moved on to the third comment.

Have you tried livinhelpers.com?

Livinhelpers? Lizina vaguely thought she had heard of it. A reply clarified, *Yeah livinhelpers has a lot of jobs where you move into the person's house. Kinda sketchy sometimes but if you REALLY need out just use common sense and you should be good.*

SAVANNAH DAWN

Lizina typed the address into her web browser. The screen that loaded was a feed of available jobs. No home page? Interesting. She started skimming through the list. This was stupid. Actually doing one of these jobs would be like *asking* to get kidnapped.

One of the locations caught her eye. Mountain's View Luxury Apartments? That place was just a couple blocks away. A high-end apartment building for high-end people.

The listing glowed softly onto her face like sunlight at the end of some long, distant tunnel.

> *15 cats looking 4 housemaid. U will need 2 cook food n wash beds regularly n other tasks as needed. pay is $1000/mo n u will have credit card 2 buy food! email at xxgizmoxx@doot.com*

She wasn't quite sure why the listing was written in such antiquated textspeak. Advanced auto-entry and spellcheck capabilities had rendered the shorthand practice obsolete. Luckily, she understood it well enough. Fifteen cats was a lot, but free rent *and* food *and* pay? Lizina paused. She considered her options. She wiped the drying tears from her face. Then she sent an email.

By the next day she had already let Pebbles know what was up, and, overall, he had been quite pleased with her handling of events.

"How many cats did you say live there?" he asked while Lizina sat on the sidewalk beside him. They had met, as always, at his holly bush.

"Fifteen." She swept her gaze left and right to make sure an inattentive bicyclist wasn't about to run over her outstretched legs.

"Hmm. Weird."

"Why?" If there had been fifteen people in one apartment, Lizina supposed she'd have thought it strange, too, but cats were a good deal smaller than people.

"It's just," he started scratching his ear, "That's an awful lot of cats to have in one apartment. I mean, cats are social, sure, but not ... that social."

Lizina shrugged. Since the only cat she'd ever known personally was Pebbles, she didn't really consider herself qualified to judge whether any particular cat's social life was normal or not. All the other cats she'd come across during her lifetime had been rather aloof, though.

"And where do they get all that money? To afford an apartment *and* a maid?" Pebbles continued.

That thought had already occurred to Lizina. Cats didn't typically have interest in high-paying careers, if they had careers at all.

"I don't know," she admitted. "They didn't say anything about it in the job ad."

"Weird," Pebbles reaffirmed.

Lizina shrugged again, though a little less nonchalant this time. The cats were verified employers—she'd even looked through some of the reviews previous maids had left them, and they were all positive. Well, almost all of them. One person had written a lengthy essay claiming that the cats had personally meddled in the former maid's personal and professional life in various improbable ways after they ended the contract, but one always found outlandish stuff like that on the internet, so she didn't think anything of it. Surely anything beyond the cats' reviews and legitimacy wasn't her business. And she wouldn't turn a chance like this down over something she could ask during her first day on the job.

Chapter 2

Ripples tilted her stomach as she stood inside the smooth, clean elevator, a bag in each hand. She'd procrastinated telling her mother and brother. Martina was still at work, and her brother had been busy doing God knows what in his room when she left with her luggage, so both would be surprised when they discovered her absence. Once her time with the cats was up, Lizina wasn't sure her mother would have her back. Lizina was supposed to bring home what little money she could so that when Gabriel graduated, they'd all have a shot at a better life. If she wasn't doing that . . . Martina might decide she wasn't worth being part of the family at all. Lizina closed her eyes, took a deep breath, and steeled herself. She would cross that bridge shortly.

Lizina took her phone out and unlocked the screen with her index finger. She opened her messaging history with her mother. Their last exchange, from weeks ago, floated onto her screen.

Are you home yet?

No I'm at the Arboretum until 6

Make sure you wash the dishes when you get home. Your brother has an exam tomorrow so I want to have a good breakfast ready.

Resentment stilled her gut's fluttering. So what if Gabriel was the "gifted child"? So what if Lizina was "challenged"? It hardly seemed right for her to give up everything for *him*. Martina may have been convinced that Gabriel was every Russo's born savior, but Lizina sure as hell wasn't.

She quickly jabbed out a text.

Got a new job, so I'll be gone for three months. See you then.

The elevator doors opened. Lizina looked up, blinking at the sudden change. She grabbed her bags and stepped into the cream hallway lit by sun-imitating lamps, glancing self-consciously to her left and right. The hallway was surprisingly short—and empty. Where one would expect a line of doors along the wall, there was only one conspicuous metal sliding door. She looked dubiously at the small finger-scanner to its left. She dropped the bag in her right hand and pulled a new number up on her phone.

I'm here, she texted.

The reply came immediately. *Gr8! Ill set the scanner to accept a new fingerprint! Just scan ur favorite finger n u can come in! Thx!!*

Ok! No problem! Lizina sent back. What a weird cat. Lizina had never met someone who insisted on communicating solely in textspeak before.

Lizina contemplated her personal opinion of each of her manual digits, then reached out her right index finger and placed it softly on the scanner. A second later, the thing chirped happily at her and swung the door smoothly open.

She was expecting a living room, or maybe a foyer. What she saw instead were soft colorful cushions and potted plants dotting a thick carpet floor the size of her mother's entire apartment. From where she stood, she could look straight out and over the cityscape through a single-pane window that covered the entirety of the back wall. Narrow stairways zig-zagged up the other two walls, where they would occasionally meet with square platforms extending out no more than two feet from the wall. Thin bridges with wooden slats connected the wall-paths to even more square platforms suspended from the ceiling in the center of the room. It was a geometric jungle Lizina couldn't even begin to walk through.

And lined all along the closest bridge were fifteen little feline faces, all staring at her expectantly.

Lizina shifted her weight back and forth between her feet. When Pebbles described his interactions with other cats, he had always emphasized the importance of propriety. She could only assume the same would apply to her. Unfortunately, she was still fuzzy on what "propriety" meant in the context of cats.

"Uh, hello," she tried. "I'm Lizina. It's nice to meet you."

The room stayed silent for a moment. Then a little orange cat sitting somewhere in the middle meowed excitedly back, "Hello!"

A small chorus of substantially less excited "hellos" followed.

"I can show you where to put your bags," a stocky black and white cat at the end of the bridge spoke in a smooth voice that sounded monotonous, but not bored.

"Thanks, I'd appreciate that," Lizina replied, trying to keep her voice mild and polite.

The cat jumped down and stretched, arching his back and spreading his white claws. Then he ambled down a hallway to her right.

Lizina awkwardly waved at the rest of the cats. The same cat that had excitedly greeted her first batted at the air with one paw in a gesture Lizina could only assume was a wave back.

She turned to follow the other cat down a hallway to her right, keeping a respectable distance to avoid tripping over him with her feet.

The maze of walkways Lizina had seen in the living room before was not present here, but there were two cat runs along both walls near the ceiling. The air smelled nice. Fresh. Not the stale, filtered air she was used to in her mother's windowless apartment at the center of the complex.

"My name is Badges," the cat broke into the silence.

"Nice to meet you, Badges," Lizina responded. She repeated the name over in her head. Big black cat Badges. It would be polite to remember all their names.

They passed several doors on their way to Lizina's bedroom. Badges let her stick her head into one of them, and she saw it was adorned with two cat-sized hammocks, matching chests, and a colorful canvas of still-wet pawprints propped up on a low easel. At the very end of the hallway, Badges turned into the room on the right.

The elaborately carved headboard of a queen-sized bed occupied the center of its far wall, next to a heavyset antique wooden desk and across from a large mounted television screen. Despite the enormity of the bed, there was still plenty of floor space around it. Lizina's black dress shoes sank into the carpeted floor.

Badges flicked his tail professionally at the double-doored closet. "You can put your clothes in there. If you have other belongings, there should be plenty of space in the nightstands and under the bed." He flicked his tail again at a door next to the closet. "There's a bathroom there with a tub and shower, so you won't have to share with the rest of us." He purred at his own humor.

"Thank you." Her voice came out airy. She felt she could *live* in this space by itself. She dropped her bags by the bed.

Badges started padding out of the room, then stopped in the doorway and turned to face her. "There's something we should discuss." He sat, curling his tail around his paws.

Lizina's pulse quickened. Generally, when people wanted to "discuss" something, it wasn't something good. She wasn't sure if it was the same with cats.

"Yes?" she replied.

Was "yes" a polite way to respond to "There's something we should discuss," or was it too informal?

Badges' demeanor remained impassive. He spoke again. "We ask very little and pay very well. We expect quality work in return." He stared into Lizina's eyes. "If we do not get what we expect, we will find someone else." He paused, as if to emphasize what he had to say next. "We also have many professional connections, more than you could guess. So if, after we have invited you into our home, you disturb the peace of that sanctuary, the consequences will be more long-lasting than a terminated contract. Do you understand?"

Lizina nodded, briefly remembering the negative review she had seen online. It suddenly didn't feel quite as far-fetched as it had before. She forced that thought out of her head and tried to calm her nerves. Equivalent exchange of goods and services. That was how capitalist economies worked, yes, and of course word got around an industry when someone was especially bad at holding up their end of a bargain. There was no reason for her to be concerned about *this* job in particular. Her nerves adamantly refused to be calmed.

The tour of the rest of the apartment was brief. The only other room beside her bedroom that did not feature cat-sized, cat-oriented furniture was the kitchen. And she was allowed to go into all of them except one.

"It's just an office," Badges explained, and left it at that.

Curiosity worked its way into her mouth, but she tasted the clean apartment air and thought of her mother—and Badges' words in the bedroom. She pressed her lips together again.

Lizina's phone started vibrating violently. She cast a desperate look of apology down at Badges and fumbled the buzzing thing out of her sweater pocket. Her heart sank. The caller ID, spelled neatly across the dome of a colorful, floating jellyfish icon, was "Mom."

Badges cocked his head up at her. "Someone important?"

Lizina faltered, staring between the jellyfish "Mom" and her new employer.

" ... Maybe," she relented, though she doubted the call could end in anything good. Already she could hear her mother's harsh voice ringing in her ears.

Badges closed his eyes and stretched his long legs out in front of him. "Better answer it, then. You've seen everything you need, I think. Settle into your room for the night and I'll speak to you again in the morning."

With that, he flicked his tail and sauntered away.

Lizina ducked her head to her phone. "Hello?" she tried in a hushed voice she hoped any nearby cats wouldn't hear.

THE COMPANY OF CATS

"Lizina Ellie Russo!" Martina's voice shrieked through the speaker. *"What* do you think you're doing!?"

Lizina hurried back to her new bedroom. "I got a new job, Mom," she said quietly.

"And what about the restaurant? What about your brother and I? You think you can just *leave* without so much as a warning?" Martina's fury threatened to spill out over the phone and onto the cats' plush carpet.

"Well ..."

Yeah, Lizina wanted to say. *Yeah*, she thought she could just leave the place where she was wanted only for her chores, whose legal authority over her had officially ended when she turned eighteen three years ago.

Martina's voice twisted frantic. "You're still sending money for rent? Your things are still here. You still *live* here."

"I don't ..." Lizina paused, plopping into the soft mattress of her new bed. She didn't want to send more money from her paychecks, hadn't planned to send more money, but the twinge of desperation in her mother's voice caught her off-guard. "I won't be living there," she continued. "I won't be eating any of the food, or using the utilities, or even taking up any space. What's there for me to pay for?"

"What's there for you to— Do you ever listen to me? You need to pay rent! We won't be able to afford it without—" Martina's pitched tone abruptly shifted back to its original aggression. "You didn't think you could use our apartment as a free storage unit for all the furniture in your room, did you?"

"Oh." Lizina hadn't considered the furniture. She'd been too caught up in, well, everything else. Guilt gnawed at her stomach in spite of herself. As much as she needed this break, as much as her mother and brother annoyed her, it wouldn't be fair, would it? And if she didn't pay, Martina might throw out all the furniture herself and repurpose the room for . . . an office or something. Then Lizina really wouldn't be able to come back, no matter what happened while she was with the cats.

"How much do you need?" Lizina's voice cracked.

Martina's voice was stern. "The same as before."

"No." Lizina almost jumped in surprise at the sound of the word coming out of her own mouth.

"No?" Martina responded, herself incredulous.

Lizina shook her head, forgetting her mother couldn't see her over the phone. "I mean, like I said. I'm not living there anymore. I'm not costing you anything; it wouldn't make sense. But— but I can give you two hundred a month. How does that sound?"

For a moment, Lizina could hear nothing but an eerie silence from her mother's end.

"Fine," Martina finally snapped and hung up the phone.

The next morning, Lizina tried to forget the previous night's phone call. Two hundred dollars a month wouldn't be so bad, especially not when she could still pocket the rest of her paycheck. Nothing to worry about.

She found it surprisingly easy to settle into an apartment full of cats once Badges had explained all her expected duties in full detail. Yes, the cats were particular and demanding, as cats tended to be, but they held no expectation for her to imitate their own eccentric lifestyles. She memorized all their names: Badges, Gizmo, Tiger, Max, Smokey, Sam, Shadow, Patch, Lucky, Misty, Charlie, Oliver, Lucy, Precious, and Midnight.

THE COMPANY OF CATS

Since almost all cleaning duties could be completed by the building's robotic cleaning systems, they mostly wanted her to cook—three meals a day, according to their very specific and individual cat tastes, and never the same thing twice—and put their dishes in the dishwasher for them. Misty, a pretty gray cat with a habit of perching in high places and looking down at everything beneath her, explained to Lizina from a ceiling hammock that cats on a whole were very self-sufficient creatures. Their only lacking attribute was that of thumbs, and so they paid Lizina. Lizina supposed that she did not mind being reduced to a walking set of thumbs as long as it meant she got free housing and free food.

The first two days, she managed. She never had been as good of a cook as Martina, who could, if given the time and materials, get lost in the kitchen for hours. Lizina considered herself more of a rice and ramen kind of girl. Martina never let her in the kitchen to make family meals, anyway.

On the third night, the cats asked her to make a pasta with a French name that had so many letters that looking at it floating around her computer screen made her want to vomit. She squeezed her eyes shut to still the motion and looked away. She could handle it, right? She knew how to follow a recipe.

Except, half an hour into making the meal, the sauce wasn't turning out quite the way she expected. She lifted a spoonful out of the pot, then splashed it back in. Watery. It should have thickened by now.

A black shape caught her eye. Badges had jumped up to watch her from the top of the kitchen island. Another tabby cat (Max?) wandered by and looked into the kitchen with poorly veiled hunger.

Badges noticed Lizina's glance.

"Is that the sauce?" he asked evenly.

"Supposed to be." She hunched away and started stirring a little more frantically. Why wouldn't it thicken?

She pulled out her phone, removing the notification for an "Are you ok over there?" message from her mother with an indifferent swipe. Martina had been sending many messages like that recently. Lizina's disappearance had restored her long absent motherly concern, it seemed. Lizina pulled up her phone's search engine. Something had to explain why the sauce wasn't thickening.

Badges jumped down from the island, then leapt up onto the counter beside her, carelessly shoving his head over the steaming broth.

He looked up from the pot and into her startled face. "How much broth did you put in?"

"A quart," she stammered.

"A quart?" he repeated, still staring incredulously.

Lizina got defensive despite herself. She resisted the urge to push Badges away from the stove and onto the ground and said, testily, "That's how much the recipe said to use."

He walked across the back of the stove to the other side of the counter where the recipe lay open on her computer. He batted up to the ingredients list.

"It says a pint," he said flatly.

"What?" Lizina rushed over to look at the screen. She stared, trying to sort out the floating list items. She picked out the word "broth." What was the abbreviation next to it? The letters kept moving. Was that a "p" or a "q" next to the "t"? Her face fell. It must have been a "p." The two letters were just so similar.

A small "oh" was all she could manage to verbalize.

Badges scrutinized her face, then turned away. As she did most of the time, Lizina found his body language indecipherable.

"Throw it out," he said, without emotion, as if his front paw had become the most intellectually fascinating thing in the room.

"Throw it out?" Lizina panicked at the thought. The broth in the pot was based on synthetic meat—and expensive. If she threw it out, she'd be pouring at least fifty dollars' worth of food down the drain.

"Well, you very well can't *use* it. We asked for pasta, not soup," he retorted.

Lizina cringed and slowly lifted the saucepan, like it might turn to jelly at any moment.

Badges' eyes slid to follow her as she dragged her feet to the sink. "Where is the fettucini?" he asked, his voice monotonous once again.

She avoided his gaze as she tilted the broth into the drain. Max slunk around the corner again with the subtlety of a hungry cat trying very hard to disguise his hunger and failing. His tail drooped with dejection when he looked up to see the much-anticipated dinner disappearing into the sink.

"I hadn't boiled it yet," Lizina responded. She avoided Max's gaze, now, too.

"May as well do it now." Badges licked a spot on his coat. "You can melt butter, yes?"

Lizina hesitated, holding back a sharp response. "Yeah, I can melt butter," she said, softly.

"Put that on the noodles, then." He didn't even look up at her.

Lizina gingerly laid the saucepan in the dishwasher. She sighed. "Okay."

Chapter 3

After that night, Lizina thoroughly pored over every new recipe. She tried to forget the reproachful voice of Badges and focus on her studies. Luckily, she did find herself with plenty of time for that—a relief after all the times she'd had to squeeze her schoolwork in between long work shifts and numerous chores. Now, the hours she spent studying brought her back to when she was very young, sitting on her father's lap with her little brother and watching her father parse through lines of code like hieroglyphs on the walls of a pyramid. Her father taught them short strings of code that did simple things, like move a little yellow square from one side of a computer screen to the next, or make it blink in place. Gabriel always learned the commands faster than Lizina, who, even back when her father was there to patiently explain the code to her, had to stare at a single line of text for five minutes just to corral all of the letters into a sensical shape. But while Gabriel was content to just let his circle slide and blink, Lizina always came back to her father, demanding to know more.

Coding was fascinating to Lizina, but it wasn't until her father brought home a small remote-control car that the joy of it truly registered with her. They made a miniature maze out of cereal boxes, kitchen spoons, and family shoes stolen from the closets. Then, for two hours, they sat together while her father gently guided her through the alphabet soup on the remote screen. This string for left, this string for right, that variable for distance. Finally, she pressed "Start" with a small, hesitant figure.

The car tottered forward as if it was equally hesitant. Then it stopped. And turned. And tottered. And stopped. And turned. And tottered its way perfectly through the constructed treachery across the living room floor. Lizina squealed. Coding, *her coding*, had transformed alphabet soup into life. And she could create again, and again, and again.

But not today. Lizina had spent the entire afternoon lying on her back in bed, trying to disentangle the swimming letters on her computer screen. And she'd still only made half the progress she had hoped for. If the thrill of creation was the addiction, then surely this—this painful headache of confused nonsense—was the withdrawal.

She heard a small voice speak up from the floor.

"Whatcha up to?"

She turned her head and saw the orange face of Gizmo, the cat who had greeted her so excitedly when she first arrived, peering up at her. Of all the cats, he seemed most fascinated by her and often asked her for her opinion on Human Things, like canned cheese and TV show characters. He was the one who had written the online ad and sent her the text messages. Her door had been closed; he had probably gotten in through the small cat door at the bottom of it. Despite their own love of privacy and personal space, the cats did not seem to understand how it applied to Lizina.

She set her computer aside. "Just studying. Do you need something?"

"Nah. Just curious." He leapt onto her bed and scrambled into her lap.

Lizina didn't mind. She indulged him by petting his head and scratching him behind his ears. He purred. His gaze followed her hand as she moved to pick her computer up again.

"Oh! Is that EvoLux?" he asked, pressing his little pink nose almost right up to the screen.

Lizina started. "Uh, yeah, it is, actually. You know it?" It had never occurred to Lizina that the cats would be remotely interested in programming. Gizmo nodded. "Badges is really good at that one." He stretched his mouth wide in a sharp-toothed yawn before tucking his face behind his paws and closing his eyes.

"Wait, do you mean that he knows other programming languages, too?"

Gizmo opened one of his eyes again, his tail twitching back and forth as he thought. "Only a little bit, I think. Other cats have that covered."

"Which other cats?"

"Oh, Midnight, Sam, Max, Misty, Patches. The smart ones, yk?"

Lizina had never heard someone say "yk" out loud before she met Gizmo, but talking with him she had quickly seen that his textspeak extended far beyond his written communication. She learned to ignore it. In any event, those were the same cats who went into the office most often. Fascinating.

"I bet he'd help you with your schoolwork if you asked," Gizmo continued. "He *loves* talking about that kind of stuff. Won't shut up once he gets going." The way Gizmo said it gave Lizina the impression that he was speaking from experience, and not necessarily a good one.

She smiled. "I'll keep that in mind."

The office that Badges had forbidden her from entering remained an enigma. Admittedly, she wondered if the cats were involved in some illegal operation, and that was why they had so much money. She couldn't very well stay employed to criminals, no matter how well they paid. The anxious thought about where else she would go in such an event then wormed itself into her stomach. She quickly brushed the feeling aside. The way things stood, it would be rude to make baseless accusations when there was a chance that the cats simply wanted privacy. She had only paid any attention to the office door when she felt she could discreetly do so. Aside from the few cats who frequented it, she had so far learned nothing about the room or what the cats did there.

"Hey Gizmo?" Lizina asked.

Gizmo chirped questioningly.

"What do you guys use the office for?" Lizina held her breath, hoping she hadn't made a mistake. Of all the cats, Gizmo was the most friendly and talkative, so he would be the best to ask, right?

If there had been any amount of risk to the question, it must have gone right over his head, because he only gave a disinterested flick of his ear followed by, "Boring cat stuff."

Assuaged, if also somewhat frustrated, by the indifferent response, Lizina continued to press. "It can't be that boring if it's cat stuff."

"Yeah, well, it is. You wouldn't be interested."

Lizina paused in uncertainty and tried to examine Gizmo's body language for clues. Unfortunately for her, she was still only very poorly versed in the art of cat-reading and didn't know what to make of the relaxed ball of orange fluff in her lap. He truly did seem indifferent to whatever was going on in the office.

Hmm.

Chapter 4

After two weeks of working with the cats, Lizina received her first paycheck. She chewed her bottom lip as she scanned her account balance. She definitely made more than she could ever hope for from a paycheck from the Arboretum. She knew she should save it, but guilt still tossed and turned deep in her stomach. She could spare $50, right?

She found what she was looking for online. She could have it shipped in an unmarked package, so she chose that option. She didn't want to bring attention to herself.

A few hours later, in the dead of the night, her phone vibrated with a notification that her package had reached its address. Sure enough, there it was when she checked the doorstep. She quietly retrieved the box and tiptoed her way through the sleeping apartment and into the kitchen.

She leaned down to rifle through one of the drawers for a knife, her nose mere inches away from the counter to better see the drawer's contents in the dim light.

A dark shadow suddenly appeared on the counter in front of her face.

"Lizina?"

Lizina dropped the package with a *thud* and jumped back in shock. Her hands clenched into fists by her sides. Then the blurry shadow reached out to tap the lightswitch on the wall, and the kitchen illuminated Max's chubby face.

"You alright?" he asked. His eyes were round with concern.

Lizina unclenched her hands and heaved a sigh. "Yeah, you just scared me, is all. What are you doing here?"

"I was looking for something to eat," he admitted. "But I saw you and got curious. I didn't mean to scare you."

She shook her head. "It's fine."

"What are *you* doing here? Were you also hungry?" he asked, leaning forward as if she might share some kind of tantalizing secret.

"No," Her cheeks acquired a slight blush. "I was just looking for a knife to open a package I got." She snatched up a knife from the drawer.

His ears pricked up. "What did you get?"

"Uh, meat broth." Lizina began to slice through the tape on the package in question, revealing the foodstuffs therein. "I thought . . ." She blushed and faltered. "I thought I would try to make the *vende*-whatever pasta I tried to make a couple weeks ago again tomorrow. For all of you."

Max leaned back and curled his tail around his paws. Maybe the mundanity of her answer had disappointed him. "That would be nice."

"I hope so." Lizina popped the broth into the fridge gel. "Nicer than last time, at least."

Max nodded.

Unsure how to react, she self-consciously gathered up the delivery carcass. "I should probably get to bed. Goodnight."

She was sitting in the big armchair in her bedroom, taking a break from deciphering a textbook to respond to yet another text from her brother asking her to clarify the proper operation of the dishwasher, when Badges called out from the cat-sized hole in her door.

"Lizina?"

"Yes?" she called back.

"May I come in?"

Badges was the only cat in the apartment who didn't simply invite himself in.

"Of course," she replied, and rapidly ran through the day's chores in her head. She thought she had finished all of them. "What's wrong?"

"Nothing." Badges walked into the room and shook his head, clearly in imitation of the human gesture. "Just thought I'd tell you that you did well on the dinner tonight."

Lizina's shoulders drooped in relief. She hadn't realized she'd tensed them. "Oh, thanks."

"I noticed you purchased the broth yourself. Would you like me to reimburse you for it?" He lifted a paw up to his nose, inspected it, and began running his tongue along the length of his foreleg.

Lizina jolted up and shook her head in earnest. "No, that's okay! I ruined the first batch; I can pay for this one."

Badges looked up and gazed impassively into her eyes. Then he returned his attention to his leg. "Very well."

Lizina sank back into her chair.

"By the way," he added. "I heard you were doing work in EvoLux?"

She remembered what Gizmo had said about Badges' enthusiasm for the field. "Yeah, it's part of my school studies."

"Really? What are you studying?" He stopped his grooming, no longer able to hide his intense interest.

"Internet security. A few more months and I'll be finished with my certificate." Her grade had dropped down to a D since the exam, and she'd have to get close to a hundred percent on every assignment from here on out to keep it from dropping further. *Hopefully,* she added, silently.

Badges cocked his head at her. "That's why you spend so much time in here, reading. All the humans I've known were more active, but this makes sense."

Lizina sheepishly fingered a strand of her hair. "Yes, well... I have a hard time sometimes. Studying takes me longer than it should."

Badges stayed silent, waiting for her to elaborate.

"I have dyslexia," she admitted. Would a cat even know what that meant? "Written letters are just... very hard to read sometimes."

Badges nodded sagely. "Misty struggles with that, too."

"Really?" Lizina's attention firmly attached itself to Badges. Cats could be dyslexic? And Misty, that was the pretty gray cat, one of the ones that apparently knew programming.

"Mhm. When she does coding, she uses a program that reads the code out loud to her."

Lizina's eyes widened. She clenched her jaw to stifle a scream of frustration, and only barely managed to keep herself from chucking her computer across the room.

Badges looked at her in concern. "Are you alright?"

Years of struggling with strings of letter after letter after—

Lizina forced a smile. "Yeah, I'm fine. Just never thought of that before."

Why hadn't anyone *said* something about this to her before? Not her teachers, not the school counselors who claimed to be "setting her up to succeed." Then again, all of the testing platforms they used blocked interference from additional programs—like text-to-speech software.

Badges twitched his ear. "You should try it."

"Don't worry, I definitely will." She jotted a note down on her computer to search for appropriate programs later. She might not be able to use it for tests, but still... maybe this would make the rest of the semester's assignments a little bit easier.

"What are you working on right now?" Badges leapt onto the armrest next to Lizina. "I might be able to help."

Lizina tilted the tablet screen to show him her textbook. His tail shot up.

Chapter 5

Two months passed quickly. Lizina was never quite sure what the cats thought of her—many of them would be friendly one day and aloof the next—but she had received no complaints since the pasta incident. School, too, went about as well as she could hope. She hadn't failed any more assignments.

Her heart sank the day she looked at her phone's calendar and saw that she only had two weeks of her contract left. She mentioned it to Badges as she was cooking the cats dinner that night.

"I guess I'll be leaving here soon," she said with forced casualness while she monitored cubes of unseasoned synthetic tuna in the frying pan.

Badges, seated on one of the stools lining the long, narrow, cat-sized dining table, paused washing his face. "You will?"

"Yeah. Only two weeks left."

"Hm." Badges stared down at his paw, flexing and unflexing his claws. "I hadn't realized."

Lizina gave the cubes a half-hearted stir. "Me neither."

"Will you go back to your mother's?"

"I was thinking ..." Lizina hesitated, "I was thinking I might try to find my own apartment. Well, a studio, at least."

"Really? Will you be able to afford that?"

"I think so. As long as I get my certificate and find the right job when I do."

"Is there anything you'd like before you go?" Badges looked into her eyes.

Lizina frowned and looked away, uncomfortable with the sudden intense attention. "What do you mean?"

"In addition to your payment. A gift, I suppose."

Lizina stopped stirring, recoiling at the thought of asking more from the cats who had already given her a well-paying job and a place to stay. "No, but thank you."

Badges paused to think. Then he asked, "Why are you so interested in internet security?"

The question caught her off guard. "Well, my dad used to work in it."

"And?" Badges' gaze remained unblinking.

Bittersweet emotions and memories had started to rise up in her that she wasn't sure she *could* verbalize, much less wanted to. She tried to give an answer that she hoped would satisfy the cat's curiosity without any further elaboration. "And ... he used to say I would be good at it, if I ever tried it." Of course, Lizina herself didn't feel particularly good at coding. Especially in recent years. "And it's a good job. And it keeps people safe."

"Used to?"

"He's dead now."

"Ah."

It probably sounded rude to say it like that. But her father was dead, and it was something that she had grown tired of talking around and euphemizing long ago. It relieved her when Badges didn't ask anything further of the matter.

"How would you like to see the office?" he asked instead.

Lizina's eyebrows shot up in surprise. "The office? Gizmo told me there wasn't anything interesting in there, though."

"Maybe not to him, but I think you'd find some interest in it," Badges answered nonchalantly.

Her old concerns about the cats' secrecy resurfaced in her mind. Was she going to get press-ganged into the cat mafia? If that was the case, she supposed she couldn't really do anything to stop it, even if she tried to say no. If it wasn't the case, she *was* curious about what the cats had been hiding back there all this time.

She decided to accept the offer. "I'd love to see it, then."

"Excellent." Badges hopped down from his stool and started walking away.

"Wait, where are you going?" Lizina urgently called out after him, her body caught between her duty to the sizzling tuna and her eagerness to follow him.

Badges turned around and furrowed his furry face in confusion. "To show you the office."

"I'm cooking dinner!"

"It can wait."

Lizina sighed and turned the heat on the stove down low enough that it would keep the tuna warm without cooking it further. As exasperating as the cat's impatience was, her own anticipation urged her along, too.

Badges slipped through the office cat door and Lizina turned the handle after him. Computer screens lined the walls above six desks barely taller than half her shin. Misty sat at one of them, staring at a screen flowing with lines of code. She didn't seem to notice Lizina and Badges' entrance through her earphones. Her paws tapped at a keyboard with keys twice the size of the ones Lizina was used to.

Lizina looked around the room in amazement. "What do you *do* in here?"

Badges licked his paw and ran it across his ear in a gesture of carelessness that failed to hide his pleased expression. "I suppose you could call it a form of cybersecurity."

Misty's ears twitched at the sound of voices. She turned around, saw Lizina, and immediately fluffed.

"Is she supposed to be in here?" Misty hissed at Badges.

"Don't worry, I let her in," he replied.

Misty's fur settled. "Why?"

"Well, I know that Lizina here is very interested in matters of cybersecurity, and since she has been doing such a superb job ever since she accepted our job offer, I thought she might like to see our operations before she leaves."

Lizina tore her eyes from the code on Misty's screen. It looked like some kind of security scaffolding. She redirected her attention to Badges. "What?" Superb job? Did they really think that?

"You might like to see what we do," he repeated.

"What *do* you do?"

Badges looked at Misty. "You're working on 43, yes? Why don't you show her?"

Misty turned back to her screen and beckoned Lizina over with her tail. Lizina obediently approached and crouched down.

"This is the code for one of Interstellar Bank's online transaction systems," Misty started to explain.

Interstellar Bank... That was an international banking corporation, wasn't it? They even operated in the Satellites.

"See this?" Misty highlighted a small patch of code on the screen. Lizina nodded. Misty continued. "This uses a Satellite system to divert .001% of every transaction to an anonymous account. That's .001% millions of dollars every day. And this isn't the only banking system we've seen affected by this code. What *I'm* trying to do is track down its source to stop it for good."

Lizina sat on her knees to better situate herself behind the cat-sized desk.

"We hack hackers," Badges quipped beside her.

Dots connected in Lizina's mind. "You're freelancers? Is this where you get your money from?"

"Mhm." Badges flicked his tail smugly.

Suddenly all the secrecy made sense. The kind of problems someone could cause with access to a system like the one in this room ... Lizina hesitated. "Why are you showing me this?"

"Like I said, you've done a superb job here. You've been very considerate, and made few mistakes. The mistakes you did make, you took responsibility for. Our background checks and informal personality assessments of you have also all turned up trustworthy. So, in return for your quality service, I'd like to offer you a favor."

The circuits in Lizina's head shorted.

"What kind of favor?" she asked.

Badges licked his shoulder. "Well, we happen to have a lot of experience in the field of internet security. I thought you might like the opportunity to do a kind of job shadow, as it were. I guarantee we could teach you a few things. Or," he continued, "I suppose I could use some of my connections to set you up with a job at an agency. Usually they like to make sure their candidates are qualified, but I bet I could pull some strings so you could get in easy, without even an interview." Badges looked up at her with soul-searching eyes. "What do you think?"

A job? Just like that? After all this work and preparation, she could just step right in, no questions asked? Lizina started to reply, then stopped herself.

But what if she really wasn't qualified? What if they let her in, and she really *couldn't* do the job? She'd be a fraud, and it wouldn't take long to expose her, either.

"I'd rather learn from you," she said slowly. "But ... this seems like very important work... I would hate to get in the way..."

"Nonsense," he reassured her.

Lizina bit her lip. Badges wasn't offering a practice exercise; this was real hacking and coding for high-profile clients. What if she wasn't good enough to keep up? How long before the cats realized that their generosity was wasted? But ... Badges had been helping her with her classes for weeks now. He knew what she was capable of, right? Nervous excitement bubbled in Lizina's stomach.

"Thank you!" she blurted.

By Lizina's standards, the cats gave their time generously and answered all her questions patiently. Misty showed her the code-reading software she used, and Lizina downloaded it on her own computer as soon as she could. If security professionals built walls to protect programs, then for the first time Lizina was experiencing cybersecurity from the perspective of a siege engine.

"How are your grades?" Badges asked as Lizina listened to a line of code for discrepancies, leaning back in a plush armchair with her eyes closed. Since the office had originally only been intended for cats, they'd had to move the human-sized chair in from a storage room.

"What?" Lizina replied distractedly without opening her eyes. The drone of code in her ears distracted her—Badges insisted there was something wrong with it and she intended to find it on her own.

"Your grades," Badges repeated patiently. "How are they? I understand most internet security companies consider them heavily before they hire someone."

Guilt pangs shot through Lizina's stomach. She opened her eyes, saw Badges on the desk across from her, then averted them. "Oh. Yeah. That's what I've heard. My grades are okay, I guess."

"You guess?"

"Most of them are good," she said, a defensive edge creeping into her voice. "It's just ..." Her shoulders slumped with defeat. "I missed an entire exam in one of my classes. It was ten percent of my grade, and I haven't been able to recover from that."

"I've never been to school," Badges admitted—this made sense to Lizina; she'd never heard of a cat attending school before, "But couldn't you ask your teacher to let you take the exam now?"

Lizina shook her head. "No. The exam locked at a specific time, and I missed it."

"Your teacher could unlock it."

"Well, yeah," Lizina said, baffled. "But he won't."

Badges remained unfazed. "Have you asked?"

Lizina hesitated. " ... No."

Badges curled his tail around his paws in what Lizina assumed to be a smug fashion. "Then ask. He can't fail you for asking."

"I suppose not," Lizina reluctantly conceded. In reality, though, she doubted it could be that simple.

Badges nodded. "Good. I expect you to do that. Have you found the discrepancy in your section of code, yet?"

Distracted by the conversation, Lizina hadn't been listening to the code buzzing in her ears. "No, not yet," she said and hurriedly pressed her eyes shut again.

Back in her room that evening, Lizina lay on her bed and stared at her computer in her hands. Badges was right; it couldn't *hurt* her grade to send that email to her professor. It could hurt her image. If everyone in the class had been subject to the same rules, who was *she* to ask for special treatment? Even if he did say yes and let her take the exam, would she really deserve the grade?

Her phone buzzed. It was a text from Gabriel. She opened it. *How do you clean the vacuum?*

The vacuum? Lizina couldn't remember the last time she'd seen Gabriel touch the vacuum, much less use it or clean it out. Last night he'd asked her for the code to the apartment dumpster, and before he'd needed help with the dishwasher. Did he have to do chores now?

She sent a quick description back, then turned her attention back to her computer. She had told Badges she would at least ask, right? And she didn't want to lie to him and say that she had if she hadn't.

She sighed. What would she even say? *Dear professor, please let me retake the exam from months ago because I missed the deadline and I'm hoping you'll make an exception for me even though you explicitly warned the entire class this would happen*—that certainly didn't make for a convincing argument. But it's not like she could just openly say, *Dear professor, please let me retake the exam from months ago because my terrible mother wouldn't let me take it.* She squinted at the blank email form on her computer screen. Could she?

Dear Professor Ogedn, she started. *Ogden,* she corrected, disappointed autocorrect hadn't worked its magic on the proper pronoun. Her cursor blinked. *I was wondering if—* no, that sounded too wishy-washy. Ogden emphasized concision in his students' programming. He probably preferred it in their emails, too. She deleted the phrase. *Could I retake the exam I missed?* That was to-the-point, wasn't it? Perhaps too much so? What if it came off as presumptuous? How could she be both indirectly polite and concise at the same time? She squinted again. No, probably not. She lightly tapped her fingernail against the computer screen. Surely describing what had happened that night would be too personal. Unprofessional. Wasn't there some kind of formal-ese for these kinds of situations? Ah, yes. *I had a sudden unavoidable family emergency, and I couldn't get to my computer until right after the test locked.* That was the terminology. Should she say anything else? There was nothing else to say, was there? *Thank you very much, Lizina Russo.*

Lizina scanned the email in its entirety.

Dear Professor Ogden,

Could I retake the exam I missed? I had a sudden unavoidable family emergency, and I couldn't get to my computer until right after the test locked.

Thank you very much,

Lizina Russo

It seemed so short. Too short. Shouldn't a professional email be longer? What would she even say? Maybe she shouldn't send the email after all. She'd just look like another desperate student begging for handouts. She'd promised Badges, though ... and he would ask her about it later. What would she say then? In the long run, she'd have nothing to lose, right?

Lizina panicked and tapped the "Send" button.

She immediately regretted it.

Now her professor would see her poorly written email and scorn her for being so conceited as to ask for special handouts. He couldn't change her current grade, sure, but he could grade her future assignments more harshly.

She gently lay her computer on her end table next to an artificial yellow daisy that bobbed in the lamplight. Then she flung herself out of bed and paced back and forth across the bedroom, planting each foot firmly into the plush carpet.

She couldn't unsend the email. She couldn't do anything now. She walked up to her bedroom window and stared out across the darkened city, lightly rapping her knuckles on the smooth windowsill.

The skyscraper the cats lived in wasn't the tallest in the city, nor did they live on the uppermost floor. All the same, this apartment was the highest vantage point Lizina had ever had. She could see the city's outskirts where they crowded up against a thick forest wall, trying to maximize their space while staying within their designated human boundaries. Streetlamps twinkled below her, and she could make out the vague shapes of people and animals walking in the streets. A small slug oozed its way out of the foliage that surrounded the window and trekked across the glass. She felt more like the slug on the window than the person on the other side of it. If she was smaller, like the slug, maybe she'd be able to find more room to fit in the world.

Her phone vibrated. She half huffed and half snorted when she saw the email.

Yeah ok

Badges, of course, was smug when she told him she'd be retaking the test. He made a big show of telling all the other cats to leave her alone during the hours of one to three PM. She would, he insisted, inevitably do fine. To celebrate her achievement, they would have a party for her the day her contract ended, which only coincidentally happened to be at the same time as the going away party the cats had originally suggested a few days ago that Lizina had politely declined.

On her way out of the party, she stroked each cat along their spine and gave them an individual goodbye. After fourteen cats, Lizina looked for Badges and spotted him trotting into the room holding a small, shiny gold object in his mouth. He set it behind him, out of Lizina's sight.

"You know," he said, "of all the human maids we've had, you've been the most interesting and the least annoying."

Lizina failed to be wholly flattered by this praise, but she tried her best.

Badges turned around and presented his small object to her. When she took it into her hands, it turned out to be a smooth laptop decal in the shape of a star.

"What's this?" Lizina asked.

"A blessing," Badges purred.

This time, she *was* flattered. She gently scratched his head. "Thank you."

Chapter 6

It turned out that she really could have lived in her bedroom at the cats' apartment, because when she opened the door to her new, empty studio, it looked to be about the same size. This was fine. Without cats to fill up the emptiness, she didn't really need the extra space, anyway. And unlike her mother's apartment, it all belonged to Lizina—paid for by the money she had saved up for the past few months. She'd be getting her program certificate in two weeks. If she could get a decent job after, she'd be able to keep the place. *If.*

She gently lay her bags down and plopped much less gently onto the bare floor beside them.

A light, insistent scratching came from the other side of the door.

Lizina jumped up and opened it wide to see the fluffy gray form of Pebbles. He let out a vibrating purr at the sight of Lizina's face.

He sauntered past her legs and surveyed the empty room. "Nice place. I'm glad you invited me to stay. No furniture?"

"No." Lizina shook her head, and bitterness crept into her voice. "Not yet. I was going to use the furniture from my old bedroom, but Mom said I couldn't have it since she and Dad are the ones who bought it. Apparently, the 200 dollars a month I was giving her was only so she could hold on to the stuff for when I came back."

"Bitch."

Lizina snorted. "Yeah. Well. I'm not going back. I made enough money with the cats that I can buy my own furniture, anyway. So fuck her."

"Indeed. But where are you going to sleep tonight?" He looked back from where he'd been circling the carpet.

"The floor, I guess."

He purred. "I'll keep you warm."

An insistent buzz from her phone woke her from her carpet slumber in the morning. Pebbles opened his sleepy eyes, still curled up in her arms. She hadn't set an alarm.

Face twisted in confusion, she reached across the floor and tugged her phone close enough to see the screen. Her brother had sent her a message. He probably needed another explanation of some chore or another.

She unlocked the phone with her fingerprint and stared at the text.

Hey. You were working for the cats living in Mountain View, ye?

Yea, she typed into her phone. As soon as she tapped the stylized paper airplane icon, the glowing jellyfish appeared on her screen with the word "SiguraCo" typed across its bluish cap.

She recognized the name, though the blatantly corporate title of the leading competitor in online security would have failed to fire a single memory synapse in the brains of most people. Of course, desperately wanting a career in the field made it Lizina's business to know these things. Badges had insisted she even send them, as well as a few other major companies, her work portfolio a week ago.

Is that why they were calling *her*?

She quickly swiped the jellyfish to the top of her phone, her fingers suddenly feeling lighter than she remembered.

"Hello?" she said in a tone of voice she hoped could be described as professionally confident. Pebbles pricked his ears up in curiosity.

"Hello." A woman's voice came clearly through the speaker. "Is this the number for Ms. Lizina Russo?"

Panic rose in Lizina's chest. "Yes," she replied. She opened her mouth again, then thought better of it and pressed her lips together instead.

The woman continued in her smooth, detached voice. "We received the portfolio you submitted. We do not usually advertise our job openings, but after reviewing your credentials and recommendations we have decided to offer you the opportunity to apply to an entry level position we have available. Would you be interested? Keep in mind, this is not a job offer, so you will have to go through the same screening and interview process as the rest of our applicants, and you are not guaranteed to get the position."

The thump in Lizina's chest upgraded to a poorly controlled skitter. Were her references really *that* good?

The woman waited patiently on the other side of the call. Pebbles started to purr.

Oh, shit. Lizina quickly decided that the exact quality of her connections didn't matter. This was like... This was like waking up to see someone had left free food on your doorstep. She had to act before it got snatched.

"Yes," Lizina said, more rushed than before, but, she hoped, still in her passably-professionally-confident voice. "I would be very interested. How would you like me to apply?"

If the woman noticed anything at all about Lizina's tone, she didn't convey it. "I can send you the details over email. What's your address?"

Lizina told her.

"Thank you," the woman said after presumably noting down Lizina's information. "Is there anything else I can help you with before I go?"

"No, thank you."

"Then have a lovely day, and good luck on your application." The woman hung up.

Lizina stared at Pebbles, stunned and slightly high from adrenaline.

"Well. That happened," she said.

Pebbles showed his teeth in a horrifying imitation of a human grin. "Congrats."

After a moment of hesitation, she asked, "Think I should tell Gabriel?"

Pebbles purred. "Do it."

Lizina followed her last message up with another smug reply. *Just got a call from SiguraCo. They invited me to apply to one of their entry level positions.*

She was pretty sure that Gabriel hadn't researched the job market for cybersecurity professionals—he was the sort who expected a job to walk up to him and introduce itself as soon as he finished the program, she suspected—but he *would* know SiguraCo.

A few minutes passed, then a small text popped onto her screen.

Did you use the cats as a reference?
Yeah

Cool.

She stared a little longer, disappointed by his lack of response. Then she turned the screen off. Whatever.

A month later, Lizina sat straight-backed in a black leather chair that was arguably comfortable—if the arguer was hoping to become a professional lawyer, and their argument was being graded on overall enthusiasm rather than credibility. Her light blue blazer and slacks creased stiffly around her crossed knees and bent elbows. This suit spent more time in her closet than on her body.

She gazed around the streamlined waiting room in a way that she hoped looked curious instead of nervous. She eyed the receptionist, a thin man in his forties, to see if he was paying any attention to her. His intense gaze on his computer screen suggested he wasn't. Behind him, a six foot screen less than a centimeter thick showed a waterfall thundering silently into a bright blue pool of water.

Lizina hadn't expected an in-person interview; online interviews were the standard for most businesses. Then again, a company like SiguraCo wouldn't be like most businesses.

She heard a door open.

Lizina swung her head to look at it and, to her disappointment, saw that it was the door that led in from outside, and not the door that led into the offices. She recognized the door's occupant with surprise. It was Gabriel.

He flashed a wide smile at her before casually strolling up to the receptionist. Lizina stared. Why was he here? *How* was he here?

Oh.

She resisted the urge to drop her head into her hands. She had told him there was a job opening at SiguraCo. Of course it would have been easy for someone like him to tweak strings until he found one that led to the position. He had connections, too.

She hoped the hiring manager was as impressed by cat hackers as she was.

Gabriel finished talking to the receptionist and flopped into a chair opposite Lizina. He looked as if he was going to say something, but before he could open his mouth, the sound of a door sliding open sounded in the room.

"Lizina Russo?"

Lizina ignored Gabriel and stood to answer the call.

The man who met her at the door wore a clean, dark purple suit with few embellishments. Streaks of gray ran through his dark ponytail. He guided her into a small conference room where more screens displayed dappled sunlight shining through bright green maple leaves that rustled in a nonexistent wind. A woman with short gray hair and a peach dress sat primly at a sturdy metal table with two empty chairs. She smiled pleasantly at Lizina. Lizina gave a restrained smile in return and sat in the chair opposite the woman. The man who had led her to the room took the remaining seat on the other side and folded his hands on the tabletop.

"Hello, Lizina," the woman spoke when Lizina had settled into her chair. "I'm Elizabeth. I'm one of SiguraCo's senior hiring officers, along with Trevor."

Trevor smiled modestly and nodded his head politely at Lizina.

Elizabeth continued. "We just have a few questions for you. They shouldn't take long. Is that alright?"

"Of course," Lizina said. She clasped her hands together tightly under the table, where she hoped neither Elizabeth nor Trevor would notice.

The questions were standard interview fare—the answers to which she had already rehearsed time and time again. It was the last question that caught her off-guard.

"As I'm sure you know, SiguraCo has many important clients, and we pride ourselves on the efficiency, security, and quality of our work. As such, we hire personnel who have a history of meeting or exceeding these qualifications. How does your training, education, and personal ethic reflect these standards?" Elizabeth glanced up from her notes.

Of course they'd want to know about her education. And, of course, they would be looking for a prestigious education. A prestigious education she didn't have.

Lizina looked at the table. Trevor and Elizabeth looked at Lizina.

"I... " Lizina faltered. "Formal education is very important. As such, I have worked hard in all of my classes." She thought of her time with the cats. "However, I have also made sure to learn as much as I can outside of class so I can see how this knowledge is used in real-world applications, which you can see in the experience I have listed on my resume."

Elizabeth and Trevor remained quiet after Lizina finished speaking, both focused on typing into their computers. Even to Lizina's own ears, her response sounded lame and unconvincing. Lizina fought to keep her face at an acceptable temperature. She suspected she was failing.

Elizabeth's fingers finally went still. "Thank you for that, Lizina. That's all we'll need for now. We just have one more thing for you to do before you go."

Wait, really? That was it? Usually when interviewers said they only had a few questions, they were, well, lying.

"We'd like to run a simulation to see how good your skills are on a practical level. You can borrow one of our computers for the exercise, or you can use your own if you prefer. We'll just need you to hook the display up to a device called SAC-3 so Trevor and I can see what you're doing."

"I can do that," Lizina said, already pulling her computer out of her bag. The gold star on its back surface glinted at her. She stood it up on the table and connected it to the device Elizabeth had mentioned. The maple leaves on the nearest display screen disappeared, and Lizina's desktop took their place. She was suddenly grateful she'd chosen a passing-for-professional image of a flowering meadow for her desktop background. She followed Elizabeth's next instructions until the screen was filled with flowing lines of security code.

Trevor spoke up. "This code is based off of a system that one of our clients used to have. If you see any flaws in the coding, go ahead and fix them."

Lizina could make up for her botched interview here. But ... there was that alphabet soup again. She stared at the screen, strings of code falling off the page like noodles. A headache started building behind her forehead. She squeezed her eyes shut. There was a better way to do this, right?

She opened her eyes cautiously. "Is it alright if I enable my text-to-speech software?"

Trevor's eyes flicked from the screen to her face with curiosity. "Go ahead."

Lizina plugged in her headphones, sat back, and listened. The immediate, effortless immersion filled her with elation.

Her thoughts wandered back to the time she had spent like this with Misty, plotting ways to infiltrate hackers' systems.

How would they have hacked this one?

There. She noticed a small patch of code. If she were a hacker, she could easily just... Without thinking, she highlighted the patch and typed in a stronger alternative. Then she kept listening.

In total, she found maybe five weaknesses in the code. During that time, neither her nor the hiring managers said a word. When the code in her ear fell silent, Lizina opened her eyes and looked over to their impassive faces.

Trevor saw her glance and smiled courteously, but without emotion. "Finished?"

Lizina nodded. For some reason, she'd been expecting a more dramatic ending to the task. Maybe a little green light, or an error message saying how many mistakes she made. But she got nothing. She hoped Trevor wouldn't notice the quivers in her body from her thumping heart.

"That's all we need from you, then." He stood from his seat and waited for Lizina to follow suit, which she did. He continued, "It was nice meeting you, Lizina. You'll be notified whether you got the job sometime within the next two weeks. I hope you have a lovely evening." He held his hand out to her.

Lizina took it, and his handshake was firm but warm. "Thank you. You, too."

Chapter 7

After the interview, Lizina convinced herself that she had irreparably botched her employment opportunity and was determined to put the whole thing out of her mind. She needed a job to keep the apartment; there'd be no point in wasting time getting her hopes up for something that wouldn't happen. And so, for the first week, she didn't—choosing to fill out job applications for a myriad of much lesser positions at other companies instead. But when the two week deadline started to near, she found herself checking her notifications more often, and compulsively listening to messages from any calls she happened to miss.

She was comparing the price of two pink secondhand armchairs online when her phone buzzed.

Lizina answered without checking the number. "Hello?"

"Lizina Russo?" It was Elizabeth's voice.

Lizina's own voice suddenly came out small. "That's me." She held her breath.

"After careful consideration, we've decided that you would make a wonderful addition to our team. When would you like to start?"

Lizina punched the air in excitement.

The first person she told was her brother, admittedly out of spite more than anything else. His response was an indifferent *Oh. Cool.* The follow up message to her mother was met with a much more testy, *They must be a small company.*

Lizina made an involuntary noise of disgust in the back of her throat, which was apparently so loud that it made Pebbles look quizzically up at her from his nap at the foot of her new bed.

"Just Mom," she explained apologetically.

He nodded and lowered his head back to his paws.

Lizina went back to her response to her mother. *No,* she tapped, *they're one of the most prestigious companies in the whole industry.*

A few minutes of silence passed before the next message arrived. *Oh, so you'll be an intern?*

No. Lizina jabbed her fingers at the screen with barely contained aggression. Martina really thought so little of her that she was now grasping at straws to try to confirm Lizina's inadequacy. *I'll have a permanent job. Where they pay me money.*

That means we'll be able to get a nicer apartment then.

Lizina stared in shock. *WE?* she finally managed to type out.

All she got back was a simple *Yes.*

No, she replied, just as simply. She was surprised to realize that she meant it, in all of its finality. Everyone she wanted to live with ever again was lying at the foot of her bed already. Except for maybe a few other cats.

She muted her mother and messaged Gizmo about her new job. He responded with a gratifying *wow! gud 4 u! congrats!* and a copious amount of exclamation points and emojis.

Thank you! :D, she messaged back.

A few minutes later, *can i call u?* appeared on her screen.

Of course!

Her phone started buzzing. A video call? She answered it.

Fifteen small cat faces appeared on her small phone screen; Gizmo's featured prominently in front of all of them. Lizina suppressed a laugh of delight.

Badges nosed his way up beside Gizmo. "Gizmo told us; we knew you would be a good fit for the job."

"Thank you!" She grinned. "You were one of my references. Did they call you?"

"Maybe." Badges flicked his ears. "Though in all fairness, we did talk to them about a second Russo, as well."

Lizina's face fell ever so slightly. "Gabriel?"

"That one. He worked for us for about a week or so. He wasn't quite as... considerate as you. Spent a lot of money while he was here and wasn't so good at keeping up on the chores. But he *insisted* we put him in contact with SiguraCo, so we did. Even gave him a chunk of code to use during the interview assessment."

A whole chunk? The only errors she saw had to be fixed with much more minute adjustments.

"Why?" she asked.

Badges flicked his ears again. "We thought he deserved a fitting reward for his quality of work." He started purring. "He must not have read it all the way through, though, because Elizabeth called us immediately after his interview to tell us he had accidently uploaded his social media feeds to the program."

Lizina recalled the highly unprofessional nature of Gabriel's social media and broke out in laughter.

Badges continued, "We knew that you wouldn't need any help."

"Thank you." Lizina's laughter petered away. "I just hope I can keep it up. This is only an entry-level position. I've still got a ways to go."

"You made it this far. You'll do fine," Badges reassured her.

"Yeah." She bit her lip, thinking of what she'd done already. "I ... I like to think you're right."

THE COMPANY OF CATS

Acknowledgements

Thank you to my thesis group members, Jack Brown and Montie Tufts, and my thesis advisor, Professor Kathlene Postma, for all of the patient critique you gave me while I was working on this project. Because of you guys, I was able to muddle my way through turning a half-formed nothing into a fully-written story. Thank you, Professor Postma, for also being the reason I knew I would be able to get a full dinner every Wednesday night in the fall of 2018 and for the occasional ride home in the dark. Thank you to Aidan, Bean, Sydney, and Nicole for letting me in when I showed up on the doorstep of your dorm in the middle of the night. Thank you to my former boss, Tiphanie Scott, for letting me "house-sit" for you when I was couch-surfing. Thank you to the Dixon family for taking me in not once, but twice when I needed a home. Thank you to Professor Alex Bove, who also gave me a ride after our class' late-night movie viewing, to Professor Bonnie Bolkan, who checked in on me when I was going through a hard time, to Professor Miranda Karson, who barely knew me but found out about my troubles and offered to buy me lunch, to Kaira Bird, who was the best peer mentor our university could have gotten, to Erica Andree, who helped me pursue possibilities I wouldn't have known of otherwise, to Justin Li, whose student support resources were invaluable, to Professor Keya Mitra, whose classroom treats helped me through days when I wasn't eating as much as I should have been, and to Professor Nancy Christoph, whose creativity helped me pass her class even in unusual circumstances. Thank you, to everyone I've mentioned and many I haven't, for all of your kindness and for brightening my days so much that I can now look back to a time full of struggle and remember it with fondness.

SAVANNAH DAWN

I made it, guys.

About the Author

Savannah Dawn is an editor and writer with a passion for exploring worlds real and imaginary. Dawn spends their weekdays doing their dream job at the public library and their weekends doing their other dream jobs—writing stories and helping others write their own stories. In their free time they make amateur art, play tabletop roleplay games with friends, read books, get distracted by the internet, crochet materials that weren't meant to be crocheted with, and start far more hobbies than they can actually sustain.

Read more at https://landloperslibrary.wordpress.com/.

Milton Keynes UK
Ingram Content Group UK Ltd.
UKHW040901181023
430840UK00004B/136